Rise and shine, small friend of mine, I hope you slept alright.
The sun will soon flood through this room, as day takes over night.

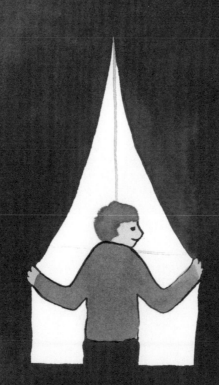

THE WORLD AWAITS

Tomos Roberts

With art by Nomoco

Farshore

A note from the author

There is a special significance to the moment we awaken from sleep. Having briefly absented ourselves from the waking world for the luxurious necessity of rest, a new day of possibility is ready to unfold. An opportunity is presented to us to go forth, act decently and to make things a little bit better. But what happens when the challenges that wait for us are so overwhelming that the temptation is to shrink away and seek refuge within the safety of the duvet?

I believe that people draw a sense of meaning from feeling like their contribution to the world matters, and from my perspective, we are living amidst a drought of true encouragement. This book was written as a reminder to myself, and anyone else who needs it, that our contribution to the world means *everything*. It is an attempt to find encouragement at a time when it is lacking. It is a celebration of the good, however small, that can be found in the places where only *you* would have thought to look.

I hope you find some encouragement in this story.

Tom

For the duo – T.R.

For Daichi – N.

First published in Great Britain 2021 by Farshore
An imprint of HarperCollins*Publishers* 1 London Bridge Street, London SE1 9GF | www.farshore.co.uk
HarperCollins*Publishers* 1st Floor, Watermarque Building, Ringsend Road, Dublin 4, Ireland
Text and illustrations copyright © Probably Tomfoolery Limited 2021 | Illustrations by Nomoco
The moral rights of Tomos Roberts have been asserted | ISBN 978 0 0084 9892 4
Printed in Great Britain by a Carbon Neutral Company

1

A CIP catalogue record for this title is available from the British Library

FSC
www.fsc.org

MIX
Paper from
responsible sources
FSC® C007454

"Go away, please not today.
I'm not going to get up.
I'm staying here,
just leave me be,
and keep
the curtains
shut."

You don't mean that! The day awaits!
It's time to shake a leg.
The world is waiting just for you,
so we need you out of bed.

"Why do you always exaggerate?
The world doesn't wait for me.
The world wouldn't notice
if I slept all day.

Please just leave me be!"

And watch you waste all that potential?
Well, that would be a sorry scene . . .

"What's this potential
you're obsessed with?

What does 'potential'
even mean?"

Okay, I'm going to tell you a secret now, but once I tell you, that is that.
You'll never see things the same again, and I cannot take it back . . .

In our core is a **plus** and **minus**,
and they're eternally at play.
They give us the power
to add goodness to the world,
or to take some good away.

Every day we plus and minus,
   with **every** thing we say and do.
      It's the difference between a careless lie,
         or the words we know are true.

You see, the global goodness number
is such a delicate amount.
And this trusted total tally
takes us **all** into account.

Whenever enough of us are **plussing,**
the global goodness is increased.

Although the **minus** lurks inside us

as a menace to the peace.

A little look
at human history
tells us all we need
to know . . .

It's no surprise

the toughest times

were when that number got

too low.

"But I'm so small and insignificant
compared with all the universe.
Why can't I just stay home in bed?
At least I wouldn't make things *worse!*"

Because you have, in you, **potential.**
It's all the plusses you could add.
It's the amount of good you're capable of,
and it surpasses all things bad.

Only you can know
how much that is
in any single day.
But if you don't contribute
what you could,

that potential fades away.

If that's the case, the global goodness slips into decline,
when one as wonderful as you forgets the value of your time.

All the things that make life special,
all the colours, sounds and tastes . . .

They lose a touch of magic
when your goodness goes to waste.

However, thankfully, for all our sakes,
the reverse is also true.
Here's what happens when you **try**
to do the best that you could do . . .

Imagine, while we're out today,
as we dodge the pavement cracks,
we spy a beetle, belly up,
and we help him off his back.

Would you still believe it wasn't worth it?
Or that nobody would care?
That you added a touch of goodness
to the world by being there.

"But that's such a tiny thing to do, you'd really get a plus for that?"

My friend, you could
plant a tree,

or make your bed,
or even pet a cat!

A word of warmth to someone struggling,
or give your grandparents a call . . .

A smile amidst a sea of frowns
could mean the difference to us all.

And though these plusses can't be seen,
I can assure you that they're real.
You'll never doubt it's working
just from **the way it makes you feel.**

And even when life leaves you weary,
somehow you'll find the strength you need.
And the global goodness grows
with each good word
and each good deed.

Imagine if we spent a **lifetime** plussing,
you just can't fathom it, my friend!
It might make a life **magnificent.**

(Although we won't know till the end . . .)

So get up now, and join me,
and let's just do the best we can.
We'll think of ways we can contribute,
we'll start today and make a plan.

And if you stumble or fall short sometimes,
try not to panic, think instead . . .

How the world got
a little bit **better,**

the moment you
surfaced from your bed.